THE STORY OF BISHOP PATTESON

This edition published 2025
by Living Book Press
Copyright © Living Book Press, 2025

ISBN: 978-1-76153-858-2 (hardcover)
        978-1-76153-864-3 (softcover)

First published in 1917.

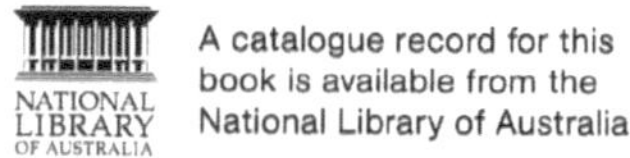
A catalogue record for this book is available from the National Library of Australia

THE STORY OF BISHOP PATTESON

by

ELMA K. PAGET

LIVING BOOK PRESS

GET ALL OF THE 'HISTORY SHAPERS' BOOKS
The Story of...

PLEASE NOTE

In this series, you will read about historical figures who displayed courage, bravery, self-sacrifice, and many other admirable traits. Their stories remind us that many people in history took bold actions and made tough choices. Yet, even those who achieved great things sometimes held ideas or pursued goals that were not beneficial to everyone. History is full of complex individuals—parts of their lives inspire us to be brave and stand up for what is right, while other parts remind us to consider the unintended consequences of our actions.

As you explore these biographies, we invite you to reflect on the qualities that enabled these figures to achieve greatness and the lessons we can learn from their mistakes. Maybe you too can become a History Shaper—someone who learns from the past and helps to make our world a better place for everyone.

CONTENTS

TO SAM

MY DEAR SAM,

Once, when you were a small boy of three up in Barbon Village, in the beautiful Lune Valley, you bought a farthing surprise packet in the village shop. Inside, we found a few chalky sweets that I was obliged to throw into the beck (but we bought some acid drops to make up), a thin tin medal of Lord Salisbury, who did so much to help govern England, and a "fortune."

This was what the "fortune" said: -

"Your heart is set on missionary work in foreign lands. You will be discouraged by your friends, but be brave and determined, and you will succeed. It will be a hard life, but the good you will do will amply repay all your toil. You will not be rich but will have sufficient money to help mankind and secure the necessaries of life."

However, when I suggest that you might be a missionary, you always agree to leave it to Paul, and when I ask Paul, he is perfectly willing to leave it to you. So, for the present, the fortune goes unclaimed.

This book is not meant to make you both missionaries. It will tell you, however, in the simple story of a good

man's life that there are missionaries who have their place in the great company of the heroes, even though they pass through the world without sharing in its praise or its rewards. And since every sensible boy was born with a talent for hero-worship, let us, when we praise great men, remember such names as John Coleridge Patteson.
Your loving,
Elma K. Paget

CHAPTER I

WHEN COLEY WAS A LITTLE BOY

A GREAT number of years ago, in 1827, a little boy was born in a long, dull street in London called Gower Street. His name was John Coleridge Patteson, but, as very few people in this world ever make use of all their names, he was usually called Coley.

Every year, things are shifting and changing and altering, as you may know for yourself if you trouble to think about it. So, as Coley was born the better part of a hundred years ago, his world was very different from ours.

King George IV was on the throne, though three years later, he died and was succeeded by William IV, who was followed, in his turn, by good Queen Victoria. Instead of our trains, trams, and tubes, four-horse coaches used to come rattling into London with cracking whips and the flourish of splendid horns. Stately ships, with their sails spread like the wings of some beautiful bird, carried you across the sea instead of, as now, our great ocean-going steamers. No cable lay curled at the bottom of the sea, serpent-like. No one had invented postage stamps — in fact, there were not very many people who wanted to write letters; and if they did, the charges were high enough to make them think twice about it. The coaches would carry the letters three miles from London for twopence and for threepence if it were as far as ten miles. Punctually at eight o'clock, the mails would start from London, the leather bags piled high upon the coach, the four horses eager to be off, while the guard sounded a merry note on his horn. Regularly, also, each evening, the postman would pass along the streets ringing his bell and calling to the people to bring out their letters ready for the mail.

> "The Postboy galloping away
> With letter-bag you'll find,
> The wharf, the ship, the lady gay,
> The beggar lame and blind,
> The boatman plying at his oar,
> The gard'ner and his greens,
> The knife-grinder, with many more
> Of London's city scenes."

That, according to a little, old, tattered book, was London when Coley was a boy — a very different London from the noisy, great city you know now.

If you think about all these things, you will see that when Coley was born, it must have taken ever such a long time traveling, and ever so much longer to hear from your friends who went away. So, for the most part, people liked best to stop safe and sound at home in England.

When Coley was three years old, his father was made

a judge. Of course, the little boy must have been pleased and amused to see the great, curly grey wig and splendid scarlet gown that his father had to wear. Judge Patteson was an honourable and God-fearing judge, respected on all sides for his just administration of the law. But in those days, the laws of England were sterner and harsher than now, and such a gentle judge must often have been troubled by the verdict or decision he had to give. Convicts were still transported out of England into her distant colonies; men and women were still punished without mercy for small thefts or forgeries; the prisons were still evil, miserable, poisonous places.

Coley had the best and dearest mother, who was usually called "Mama," two sisters, and a brother, with whom he played and with whom he quarreled. For, like a good number of boys, Coley had a temper. He could scream, kick, and pinch, and even try to stab his sister Fanny with a pencil. "Mama" had her hands full to keep the peace.

Lessons were learned each day with a governess named Miss Neill, whom all the children loved and who was to remain one of Coley's best friends all through his life.

When he was five years old, he could read, and his father gave him a Bible for his birthday present. Coley loved spelling out the great, solemn, beautiful words, even though he could hardly understand what they meant. He used to think, in his own quaint little way, that he would almost like to be a clergyman when he grew up because he thought that he could make so many people happy when he read the *Absolution* or Forgiveness of Sins.

Although, as you know, it was difficult and lonely work at that time to travel into far countries, a cousin of Coley's had gone out to be a missionary bishop in the island of the Barbadoes. One day, a great hurricane swept over the islands, breaking down the houses and churches and rooting up trees. This quite took Coley's fancy when he heard of it. Here was a land of adventure better than all the Gower Streets in the world. Off he rushed to "Mama," crying out, "I will be a bishop, and I will have a hurricane!"

When Coley was eight years old, he had to go to school, and, like most other boys, he did not in the least want to go. Still, the school was in the country, away down in Devonshire at Ottery St. Mary, where his grandfather lived, so that it must have had some advantages. Ottery St. Mary is a very happy place for a boy who loves the country. There are great, wide-spreading trees that open their arms as if they were stretching in the warm, soft air. There is a river whose very name — the Otter — must speak to boys of early-morning hunting, when the dew still hangs upon the grass and the sun is up but not yet warm, as is very often the case with the boys themselves. The grave church stands like a mother with the little town at her knee, and, if you climb to the hills and the heather, you look away to the sea, which has called and is still calling to so many Devon boys.

Notwithstanding all this, Coley wrote a very miserable little letter to his father and mother:

"I can never be happy till I have left college, except in the holidays. School is a place of torment almost to me, but I must go to school some time or other, or else I shall never be a judge, as I hope to be some day. To think of you all makes me *chry*. I believe you will not mind that blot, for it was a tear just before it fell."

All the same, Coley got on very well and was particularly good at cricket, riding, and running races; and there were few things he enjoyed more than the fireworks on the 5th of November. Above all, his younger brother James soon joined him at school, so he was not lonely anymore. He loved to get leave from school to go and see his grandfather and granny at Heaths Court, partly because he was an especially loving little boy, partly because most little boys like play better than work. One day, Coley wanted to go to Heaths Court so badly that he told his master a number of fibs in order to get leave. Fibs are usually found out very quickly, and they are even more uncomfortable and unpleasant when they are not found out. However, the master very soon discovered that Coley had not spoken the truth, and, for a little while, all the pleasant leave was stopped, and, as a punishment, the little boy was kept prisoner in the school courtyard. At which, he was very miserable and very sorry, and wrote a long, pitiful letter to say he was the worst boy in the world, but he meant to try and be better.

CHAPTER II

COLEY HEARS THREE SOLEMN VOICES AND GETS INTO THE CRICKET ELEVEN

IN 1838, when Victoria had been Queen of England for nearly a whole year, and when Coley was eleven years old, he was sent from the school at Ottery to the great and famous school of Eton. Everyone has heard of that marvellous old place, that teaches and trains its sons, and then sends them out into the world to teach, work, and rule. The beautiful red–brick buildings and grey, uplifted chapel seem almost to rise out of the calm, wide river Thames. High above the river and the school, the great castle of Windsor lifts itself up like some wise, wakeful giant who has to guard the small people hurrying about his feet.

Coley was a very little boy to go to Eton; the young girl up at the castle was very young to be Queen of England. Perhaps the little boy looked up at the castle and longed to serve the girl who lived within; perhaps the girl looked out of her windows across the meadows and longed to play and amuse herself like the schoolboys who had no cares of state.

One day, when the young Queen was out driving, the cheering and excited crowd swept round her carriage, carrying little Coley forward with the rush and pressing him right under the wheels. He must have been run over if the Queen had not stretched out a royal hand to save her small subject.

Two years afterward, the Queen was married, and the Eton boys decked themselves out with white favours and white gloves; which, undoubtedly, show us that Eton boys were very nice and proper in those days. But when the 5,000 lamps were alight on the triumphal arch, when the news sped of the arrival of the royal pair from London, even the white gloves proved no hindrance, and away rushed the boys, shouting, pushing, and cheering. They only paused now and again on their way to the castle to give a runaway knock at the houses they passed. Of the 550 Eton boys, only two were able to force their way into the great quadrangle of the castle, but Coley was one of the two.

He ends his letter of excited description with a little outburst of rejoicing: "I was so happy!"

Cricket, bathing, and boating were the chief delights of Coley's life. Now and again, he worked hard at his lessons. Now and again, he did nothing of the sort, with the result that he got unsatisfactory reports and became very miserable, and then had to set to work again with better pluck and determination.

While Coley was enjoying all the fun and happiness of Eton life, three solemn things happened to him. They came like three voices calling to him to see if he were beginning to get ready for a life of hard, unselfish work as well as the life of play. They tried and tested him as you try the ice to see if it will bear.

The first voice was a sermon.

One Sunday morning, when Coley was fourteen, he went off to New Windsor Church to hear George Augustus Selwyn, first Bishop of New Zealand, preach. A bishop sounds as if he must be very grand; a man with a big house, a big gold ring, and perhaps a gold cross hanging round his neck. Bishop Selwyn had none of these. He had no palace to go to, only a nice home in England to leave behind. He was going to plant the good seed of the Word of God in the strange, little-known world of islands, where he would find a few English colonists and any number and every variety of heathen, savage tribes. The bishop was well known in Windsor, and as he spoke, the people in the crowded church listened and wept, for they could not bear to let him go. Coley, unable to get a seat, stood the whole time. He also listened and listened.

It was the first Voice speaking very gently to him.

A little while after, during his holidays, the same Voice spoke again when the bishop, in saying good-bye to Lady Patteson, added, "Will you give me Coley?" Coley's mother did not answer. Perhaps she had heard the Voice too.

The next Voice to call Coley was his Confirmation, when he knelt before the bishop to receive the gift of the Spirit and to give himself to God. He had been working hard at school, and he had climbed to a good place, besides getting a great deal of praise for his Latin verses.

Coley had grown thoughtful; he was not a bit afraid of being serious when there was anything worth being serious about. He read his Bible with some other boys in his room, but as he was very shy of being considered good, he kept an open Shakespeare on the table and a drawer into which he could slip his Bible if anyone happened to come into the room. At the Confirmation, the bishop spoke to the boys about the noble self-denial of Bishop Selwyn, and Coley kept the saying in his heart.

The third Voice to call Coley was a great sorrow. He was called home from Eton to see his mother, who lay dying. It must be very hard to kiss your mother for the last time.

These are grave things to tell you, but Coley was preparing for a grave work.

Above all other things, Coley wished to get into the cricket eleven and play for Eton on Lord's cricket ground. In those days, the ground was neither so large nor so grand as at present. The boys could see and recognize, from their places in the field, the friends who rode or drove to the ground to see the match.

Coley first got into the eleven in 1843 and went up that

summer to play in the two great matches at Lord's — the Eton v. Harrow and the Eton v. Winchester. Perhaps the celebrated cricket professional Lillywhite was there to watch him. Certainly, once at Eton, Lillywhite got quite cross because he could not bowl Coley out.

Coley did especially well at Lord's his second year. He was sent in first in the Harrow match, and it was all he could do to keep up his wicket against the straight, steady bowling. However, he scored fifty runs with only one hit for four and quite broke the bowling, so that Eton won easily. Coley made a brilliant catch at point, which got the last Harrow man out.

Then came the Eton v. Winchester. Though all went well at first, the Winchester captain played an uphill game so finely that it almost seemed as if his side must win. Then Coley and the Eton captain had a great consultation about the bowlers, and, at last, Coley's advice was followed. Though the match was a very close one, his advice won the game. Depend upon it, Coley slept soundly that night; for there is no success like a boy's success when he saves a match for his school.

In another and less popular way, Coley had to help the school. Once every year, the cricket eleven and the eight of the boats met at dinner at a hotel in Slough. Bad habits will grow up in school like ill weeds in a garden, and it was the custom at these dinners to sing songs that were neither good to sing nor to hear. Coley would not hear them. "If that doesn't stop," he called out, "I shall leave

Lillywhite could not bowl Coley out

the room." The boy went on with the horrid, vulgar song, and Coley got up and, with a few others, left the room.

Of all the good things that fall to the fortune of an Englishman, cricket is perhaps the best; but there may come a time when even cricket must be sacrificed. So Coley wrote to the captain of the eleven to tell him that unless an apology were made, he must leave the eleven. They sent the apology at once, and the songs were never sung again.

The time at Eton was drawing to a close, but the last term was to add just one more happy victory to those delightful school days.

Coley shall tell you about it himself, in a letter written home: -

"You may suppose I was miserable at leaving Eton. I did not, I assure you, without thanking God for the many advantages I have enjoyed and praying for His forgiveness for my sin in neglecting so many. We began our match with Harrow yesterday by going in first. We got 261 runs by tremendous hitting; Harrow, 32, and followed up and got 55: Eton thus winning in one innings by 176 runs — the most decided beating ever known at cricket."

CHAPTER III

COLEY WEARS A BLACK COAT AND GETS TO WORK

T HERE are a good many people in the world who take everything very much as they find it, without asking any questions. Now it is wise to look well at a question to see if perhaps it has another side; for it usually has, and sometimes a very ugly one too, that must be faced if you are to do any good in the world.

Coley, grown tall and broad-shouldered, with as tough muscles as cricket, boating, and all sorts of exercise could give him, went up to Oxford and found himself very happily settled at Balliol College. He brought to Oxford a good many things. He had a name and a fame as a capital cricketer and a capital companion; he brought a certain amount of praise for his book learning and a real talent for learning languages. Besides this, he had made up his mind to take a good look all round a question before he tried to answer it. This is sometimes called the power of judgment and was a good thing for a judge's son to possess.

The first question he had to answer was about as difficult as any that ever came to him. Directly he got to Balliol, he was asked to play cricket for Oxford and offered his blue. There must have been some stronger power at work behind Coley's mind that even made him hesitate before answering "Yes" to such a tempting offer. You may be sure his Eton coat and cap were in his box when he came up to the university; he had, without doubt, the bat that scored those fifty runs at Lord's, and he was as safe a catch and as good a point as anyone could desire. All that! And yet Coley said "No." For above and beyond the joy of cricket, there was forming in his mind a wish to work, to grasp out and get something bigger, stronger, firmer — something that would last forever, that would be of use to other men. He looked quite simply at the chance of playing for Oxford and refused it because it would cost too much money and take up too much time.

Every one knows the story of the dog with eyes as big as saucers who guarded the pennies, and the dog with eyes as big as soup-plates who looked after the silver, and the dog with eyes as big as windmills (he was a terribly fierce fellow) who had care of the gold. And how the brave little soldier came and stuffed his pockets full of pennies, and then threw them away for the silver; and, coming to the third dog, whom he hardly dared approach, he at last gathered up courage to throw away the silver and pack his pockets full of gold.

It was rather like this with Coley at Oxford; he had got

as far as the soup-plate dog and had thrown away the pennies to get silver in exchange.

Never, however, did Coley cease to regret those most delightful years at Eton — never had the old school a more faithful son, never was it more passionately loved. "To stay at Eton in the summer is paradise." That is Coley's written opinion.

At last, when the time came for Coley to leave Oxford, he had to make up his mind what he would be. He had done as well at his books as anyone had expected, he had got a Fellowship at Merton, and he was twenty-two. In the old days, he had wanted to be a judge, but he had changed his mind and had made the dull choice of wearing a black coat and becoming a clergyman.

If you tell your cherry-stones, as every sensible person does who has the chance of a helping of cherry tart, you probably say: "Soldier, sailor, tinker, tailor, rich man, poor man, beggar-man, thief." And they all sound very interesting professions, except perhaps the poor man. You could be a splendid soldier, a daring sailor, a traveling tinker, perhaps a political tailor, or a rich man to do as he pleases. A beggar-man, if he is a tramp, sees a good deal of the world; and as for a thief, why, you could be a second Dick Turpin!

But a clergyman! He isn't even mentioned in the cherry-stone fortunes; and if you are a clergyman, it means, or ought to mean, that you write that difficult word "Self-sacrifice" right across your life.

It was another question to look at before Coley could answer. But this question always puts its ugly side to the front, and when you look all around it, you see the real beauty that it possesses. For the other side of the question is feeding the hungry, clothing the naked, visiting the sick, helping the prisoners, and teaching the ignorant. So Coley made his choice, and on September 14, 1853, he was ordained in Exeter Cathedral and started work immediately afterward as curate of Alphington, a little village two miles from Feniton Court, where his father now lived.

Coley began work with a good store of books, and they were not quite all sermons and Bible lessons. He was to live in the country, and so he was determined to learn all he could about the country. He bought books about farms and allotments, which are the little gardens given to the cottagers. He studied dairy work, digging, and gardening; he read about cottages and village schools — everything, in short, that might help and interest his cottage neighbors.

He started a lodging house for farm boys; for all his life long he loved to get hold of boys and to give them the best sort of games and books, teaching and training.

All this while, Coley had a pleasant time with the dog with the soup-plate eyes, and he had collected plenty of silver instead of the other good things he had given up. Now came the time to throw away the silver and to make the acquaintance of the fierce-looking fellow who guarded the gold — to pass on from better to best.

Bishop Selwyn, who, you will remember, went away from Windsor to New Zealand, came home for a holiday and went, of course, to stay at Feniton Court.

August had come, and the country round Ottery, Alphington, and Feniton was looking its very best. All the gardens were bright with early autumn and late summer flowers, the ripe fruit hung heavy on garden walls, the bees droned lazily and pleasantly, while away in the fields, harvest had begun, and the reapers were busy with their scythes.

It was stay-at-home holiday weather, and Coley walked off to Feniton Court to breakfast, full of his plans and his work, and eager to meet Bishop Selwyn. After breakfast, Coley and the bishop walked out into the garden. Shady leaves and green lawns, and the bright flower beds, with a blue sky overhead — what more could he want? And yet the bishop looked at Coley, and right through Coley, and he said to him, "Are you satisfied?"

Now then, Coley, are you ready to throw away the silver and stretch out your hands to grasp the gold?

He hesitated a bit and said, "Yes," and "Well, *perhaps* not quite — and *perhaps* one day he would go and work in a big town — or perhaps he would be a missionary."

"If you wish to be a missionary," said the bishop, "you must be a missionary now, while you are young and well and strong. You must be willing to go wherever you are sent. Would you be willing?"

Then Coley threw away the silver of his happy home life, and grasping the gold of a big self-sacrifice, he answered, "Yes."

What about his old father, the judge? What did he say when Coley told him of this strange new wish that was driving him away from home, out into the world beyond? Judge Patteson had always been an honest, simple, upright judge. He took Coley's wish and set it before him and tried it and tested it as a good judge should. As the evidence and the reasoning grew clearer, and the judge saw more plainly what his verdict must be, his heart grew sadder, for his love was great and true, and Coley was his own dearest boy.

Then the judge spoke, and he spoke bravely. "I give him wholly," he said, "not with any thought of seeing him again. I will not have him thinking he must come home again to see me."

The drums beat and the pipes sing with their shrill, excited voices, and all the world is cheering when Red Coat marches away. But when Black Coat gets his marching orders, there is no band and no excitement; only here and there, in quiet English families, father, mother, brother, or sister grow grave and go silently about their work, for the great sorrow and the great pride have come into the house. "He has been wanted for a missionary," they say, "and we have had to let him go."

CHAPTER IV

COLEY SAILS IN THE "DUKE OF PORTLAND" AND LANDS ON THE OTHER SIDE

O N March 28, 1855, Coley set sail for New Zealand in the *Duke of Portland.* The ship swung round with the tide at five o'clock on the chilly afternoon, and then gradually the figures of those who watched on shore grew smaller, the straggling houses of Gravesend faded away, till, at last, England — and that is the worst good-bye of all — disappeared into the gathering darkness, and they were gone. Now, beside the ship's company and Bishop Selwyn's company, there were a great number of emigrants who were leaving home and England forever. There must have been a terrible lot of sadness aboard the big ship, and it must have seemed to Coley as if Eton, and cricket, and Feniton, and the jolly old days, were far and far and far behind as he settled himself in with the strange, sad company.

When you don't know, you don't care, and there is no

harm in not caring when you do not know; but at last you have to learn about some of the sorrow in the world, and then it is very tempting to say, I won't know, and to stop up your ears and run away. Coley, being brave, determined he would know and understand trouble as well as happiness, so he did all he could on the voyage for the lonely, disappointed other people.

Fair weather, fine weather, and foul weather met them as they moved slowly on their way. There were new things to see every day — the new stars at night as they went round the world, the flying fish about the ship, the odd lights upon the water, or the great marvel of an iceberg. Coley had also plenty to learn. It had already been settled that, for the future, six months of the year should be spent in sailing about amongst the distant South Sea Islands, so he had hundreds of questions to put to the sailors about the ship and her management. Whenever he could find an opportunity, he was learning, watching, and even helping to sail her.

Then, too, there was the great difficulty of learning the languages — don't miss out the last s, for it was not one language he had to master, but as many languages as there are islands in the Southern Sea. You have no idea what difficulties missionaries have about learning languages. If we set about learning — or rather, if other people insist that we *should* learn — Latin or Greek or French, orders are sent to the booksellers for grammars and dictionaries and easy reading books, and the lessons start. But in savage lands there are no grammars and no books and no writing, unless it be in letters you do not understand. Missionaries have to listen and guess and find out and write it all down, so that in the end they can give the natives the best two gifts that it is in the power of man to give — and these are the knowledge of God and a written language.

Other missionaries and Bishop Selwyn himself had already done a good deal of such work, so that Coley was able to learn even on the voyage out how to talk to some of the natives amongst whom he was going to live.

Once during the voyage, the *Duke of Portland* had to weather a tremendous gale. Great seas broke over her decks, sweeping them almost clear and breaking through the bulwarks. The wind whistled and screamed through the ropes, and sea and rain seemed to meet in a perfect whirlpool over her. Coley was tossed hither and thither in his cabin and could only stand for a few moments on the deck to watch the great storm. The ship, unable to make any progress, lay to and drifted with only two or three small sails set. Poor emigrants, and poor Coley!

There is an end to all things, and even the long voyage was finished at last. What a good sight it must be to see the cliffs and crags rising up on the horizon instead of endless, unbroken sea! The weather was beautiful, the wind, though a little bit contrary, was light and pleasant, and there, lying out upon the ocean, was Coley's new world.

Coley on board the *Duke of Portland*

"Anyhow," said the bishop, "you are a good sailor, and that is one great point decided."

Then came the bustle of landing — the reappearance of all the odd, sad bundles and packages that the poor emigrants had brought away with them, the eager curiosity to see all that could be seen, the busy work of the sailors as they sped to and fro.

Depend upon it, Coley had only eyes for those strange dark figures that crowded to welcome and to gaze — his first sight of *Maori*, whose dusky forms stood out so mysteriously from the golden mimosa trees and flowering shrubs.

"Tena na ko koa i noa?" cries Coley as he holds out his hands to grasp the brown ones in friendly greeting, and that means the best possible New Zealand "How do you do?" and he said it with all his heart.

Very soon, the Maori had learned to call him "Te Patihana," the nearest they could get to Patteson, which was really his name if you care to look back to the very beginning of this book, though it is nicest to call him Coley still.

You must not fancy the Maori were savage people, for even though this all happened so many years ago, they had, for the most part, become gentle and kindly under the influence of true religion, even though they were not all Christians. Their quaint, tattooed faces were bright with pleasure as they saw Bishop Selwyn, and they cried out, "Eh te Pikopa," and danced round him, clapping their hands. In England, we see crests and coats of arms on silver or notepaper or carriages, but in New Zealand, the Maoris wear their crests on their faces, and all sorts of family history, which you and I could not understand, may be found tattooed upon them.

Coley was soon taken to St. John's College, Auckland, which was to be his first home.

In those days, a solitary path winding across the wild, uncultivated bush led to the college; the seven miles between it and the little town of Auckland were quite deserted, except for a few stray horses belonging to a native chief named Paul. Once arrived, Coley was given his own special room, where he could unpack his possessions and look away across the harbour and the sea. In the room itself, he had just a bed, a table, and a bookcase: perhaps it all looked rather empty and unfriendly now that the excitement of arrival was over, and he had time to miss the people he loved so well in England. Of course, he was glad to have got there, yet it is hard to arrive without the old familiar welcome of home, hard to realize that father and sisters could never be at the journey's end.

CHAPTER V

COLEY'S SHIP, THE "SOUTHERN CROSS," STARTS FOR THE ISLANDS

SOMETIMES the diocese in which a bishop works is called his see, but in Bishop Selwyn's case you might very well have called it his sea, for his business lay in the great waters, amongst countless small islands, inhabited by any number of different tribes. Neither had he small distances to cover. Norfolk Island, with its strange history of convicts and marooned sailors, which you must read about some day in other books, was 600 miles away from New Zealand, and Norfolk Island was only the beginning of the islands of Melanesia. You may well imagine that the bishop had to learn a great many things that other bishops need take no account of. He must understand how to be bishop of his diocese and captain of his ship; he must know how to make clothes and to cook, how to build houses and how to doctor sick people; and all the while he must be as brave as the soldier who takes his life in his hands and marches coolly into real danger.

First of all the bishop had a little ship to manage called the *Undine*, but his needs and his work grew out of that as you grow out of your clothes. Then came the *Border Maid*, and a very willing maiden she proved, until she grew too old for further service, and the bishop began to long for a ship of his very own, built for himself, made for his work, a real mission ship for the South Seas.

And his wish came true. For after many delays and much anxiety the good ship *Southern Cross* was launched from Southampton on the very day that Coley left England. The Southern Cross! You have heard that, as Coley travelled round the world, he saw strange stars appearing in the sky at night, and amongst those stars the Southern Cross is the most beautiful and the most distinct. What better name could be found for Bishop Selwyn's mission ship? For the thought of a star always conjures up the coming of the three kings and the:

> "Star of wonder, star of night,
> Star of royal beauty bright,
> Westward leading, still proceeding,
> Lead me to the Perfect Light."

Now the bishop's plan had been to cruise about among the distant islands, making friends with any well-disposed natives and persuading them to come with him in his ship away across the seas to Auckland in New Zealand, where he could teach them for a little while before sending them home again. In this way, a great number of the natives would learn about God, get a little ordinary education, and gradually understand that the missionaries wished to be kind. Then, on their return home, they would carry good reports about the white men who wanted to make friends.

But other people besides missionaries were busy on the Southern Seas. The days of pirates were over, and yet an ugly new sort of pirate was busy in those parts. Ships that looked like the Southern Cross plied their trade in the same waters. Yet if kindness and love reigned on one ship, greediness and unkindness were master of the others. For the white traders came to the islands with friendly messages and tempting offers, and then, suddenly seizing the opportunity, they carried off the poor ignorant natives as slaves to this land or the other. Very often in the final struggle some of the natives were killed, or sometimes they were bribed by drink (which the traders brought with them), or even made intoxicated, before they could be carried off.

The good ship *Southern Cross* had, therefore, enemies in the South Seas.

Besides these white traitors, there were real dangers amongst the natives. Coley would not only have to be on his guard against these new sorts of pirates but would have to be watchful of the cannibals. The very name is exciting.

We can hardly put into words the dreadful thought that men should ever eat each other, but yet such a thing is true. At the close of a war between the tribes, the prisoners would be slaughtered and used, with ferocious and horrid glee, in the feast of victory. It is better not to talk or write much about such things; that is what happened, and amongst such people, Coley had chosen to live.

After a little experience up and down the difficult New Zealand coast, Coley had become a first-rate skipper and was as much at his ease with quadrants, compasses, and ropes as he had been in the old days with cricket bats. The joy of the sea and seafaring life had captured him. Even when not cruising, he still lived aboard; the noise of many waters lulled him to sleep, the stars watched him from overhead, the winds sang and hummed in his ears, and Coley, in his narrow canvas bed, slept and dreamed of home as if no wide ocean separated them.

The first year had nearly passed. The *Southern Cross* had been proved and tested, and Coley had been proved and tested too, when the bishop finally made up his mind to start forth on his voyage to the distant islands.

Ascension Day was chosen for the start, the day when the Gospel rings out its "Go ye and teach all nations, baptizing them in the name of the Father, and of the Son, and of the Holy Ghost." They had a capital crew of five, a friend named Leonard Harper, bishop and Mrs. Selwyn, besides Coley, on board. Once more there were the good-byes, and the exchange of a friendly land for a limitless ocean, but by this time Coley was almost more at home in his little cabin than anywhere else. His seamanship was taxed to the uttermost very soon after the start, when once again they had to go through the experiences of a wild and terrible gale. The whole sea was one drift of foam, the spray was driven in clouds about the ship, and sea after sea dashed itself relentlessly against her bulwarks. "Water, water, everywhere," rushing down the companions and hatches, sweeping the decks, until Coley gasped for breath, and was almost unable even to open his eyes. Once more the little party was brought safely through their danger, and the next day, amid heavy surf, the bishop and Coley were able to row into Cascade Bay, Norfolk Island.

The first person to meet them was a convict who had been left on the island to welcome the men from Pitcairn Island, who were to arrive in a few days. These Pitcairners had a strange, romantic history. They were the descendants of the mutinous crew of the ship *Bounty*, who had cast their captain and nineteen other persons adrift in an open boat towards the close of the eighteenth century. The sailors themselves had settled on a small island, where they had intermarried with the natives, and under the rule of John Adams, one of their number, had gathered together a little colony of forty-six persons. Having outgrown Pitcairn Island, the English Government allowed them to form a colony on Norfolk Island, where they were now expected. Coley had already begun to delight in the tropical climate, and his first impressions were all that he could have wished. The island was fertile and more or less civilized. Oranges, lemons, potatoes, and English vegetables were all well established, while the native trees, called the Norfolk Island Pines, grew to a magnificent height and size. Besides, it is pleasant to stretch yourself after a long and not very comfortable voyage, and we can fairly leave Coley for a bit to find out a little more about the other islands.

CHAPTER VI

COLEY STARTS FISHING IN STRANGE WATERS

LYING on the breast of the endless ocean, you may find the enchanted islands. Blue above you, blue around you, and the murmur in your ears of a sea that breaks without ceasing on the distant reefs. Far away to the east, west, north, and south, you can see islands. Here, a volcanic peak rising like a cone out of the water; there, a group of palms that seem as if they had been placed in the water as you might arrange roses in a glass bowl. Seabirds cry to one another from the quivering blue of the sky or the moving blue of the sea; there is the scent of sandalwood and rare perfumes hanging in the air.

In this sea-world, there are strange powers at work.

Out of the clear water, enchanted flowers are pushing their way, as snowdrops struggle through the hard ground. Slender fronds grow and branch in all directions, but so silently and gradually that the sea hardly knows they are there. Yet one fine day, a great barrier of coral will succeed in driving back the waves, and instead of a stem here and a coral flower there, a reef has been formed and a new island made. Sometimes these coral islands lie like fairy rings upon the water, sometimes a barrier that stretches, now above, now below the water, for hundreds of miles.

What sort of flowers are these that you can string round a baby's neck, and that yet have the power to defy the sea?

They are the marvelous work of myriads of tiny creatures, who live and labor and build, and start a thousand new colonies to live and labor and build in their turn. Never was such industry; never were such workers. No difficulties are too great for them. Even when the sea breaks off their flower-like homes to dash them away, they only start a new colony and a new reef wherever the tide and the waves may take them. White coral, pink coral, red coral, branching and building, with palms and flowers stretching down to meet them, and the trembling tropical heat filling the air. Truly, if good Saint Brendan found the enchanted islands, he must have found them there.

But alas! Behind the palms, within the coral reefs, strange people come and go, moving like dark shadows across the brilliant picture. Hatred and war are in their hearts as they fashion their arrows and tip them with deadly poison. Wild, untamed beings, who look across the sea, ready to greet chance strangers or foreign ships with a thousand war canoes that dart out like angry bees, with their arrow-stings ready for action. Such glittering and beautiful canoes are these, laden with hatred and death! Mother-of-pearl gleams out from their sides; the prows tower from the water in strange, fantastic shapes; garlands of flowers hang round and about them.

These dark, gloomy figures make Melanesia more than ever like a fairy tale. It is as if some dreadful shadow had swept across the most brilliant transformation scene that ever delighted an audience. Shut your eyes and picture the beautiful colors again, until you can almost fancy that a butterfly's wing has brushed across the page and left its flashing tints behind. Then you will decide at once that a good fairy is wanted immediately to touch the dark shadows with a wave of her wand, so they may be turned into princes and princesses, worthy of their fair and gracious isles.

The fairy has started, and he is getting nearer every day; that is to say, if you can call Coley a fairy—great broad-shouldered man that he is, with hard, athletic muscles, and a merry smile that would make you fond of him at once. He has no magic wand, but a Power beyond himself, that can draw the royal white spirits from the poor dusky bodies.

Coley was to work among five special groups of islands, and though it is rather like a geography lesson to try to learn their names, it may perhaps help to make the history of his work clearer.

Six hundred miles, or more, to the north of Norfolk Island there were the Loyalty, New Hebrides, Banks, Santa Cruz, and Solomon Islands. Of these, the Loyalty Islands were the least dangerous, as the people had already been taught some idea of the faith by native teachers from Samoa. No sooner are the Loyalty Islands left behind than you enter at once into the zone of danger. Already some teachers from Samoa had been murdered by the natives of the New Hebrides group of islands, and the shadow of Death was hanging over the Scotch missionaries whom Coley found at work in Erromango. Like a dream-island on a dream-sea, you come to Faté, with its woods, beautiful beyond words, creeping down the coral rocks to meet the sea. Crystal clear is the water, and birds and butterflies flash out wonderful colors as they dart among the palms. Yet this fairy place is the grim scene of the murder of the shipwrecked crew of the *Royal Sovereign*, that had its terrible ending in heathen dance and cannibal feast.

Beyond the New Hebrides, we come into the glamour of the Spanish Main. The island names here conjure up few pictures of dusky Melanesians but speak to us of Spanish dons and hidden treasures, as we say over to ourselves such titles as Santa Cruz, San Cristoval, Espiritu Santo, Guadalcamar, or Santa Maria. We can fancy the Spanish ships riding at anchor in these pleasant waters in the days when Elizabeth ruled England, and the spirit of adventure was abroad. The gaily-painted sails flapped lazily in the wind, with their devices of Saint or Virgin speaking a better mercy than the dons were wont to show. The natives had learnt to stammer out the word "amigo," the Spanish word for friend, and for long made some effort to trace the sign of the Cross, that had been taught to them by Doña Ysabel, whose brave Spanish husband, Don Alvaro di Mendana, had founded a colony on San Cristoval in 1594. In such islands as these, we want to forget all about missionaries and think only about doubloons and bar-gold; though, indeed, no treasure awaited the Spaniards, however confidently they set forth to find it.

These "soft meandering Spanish names" set our fancies off and away with *Amyas Leigh*, and such heroes of old days. But the Spaniards, and the treasures, and the romance had gone this many a long year. They had left little behind except a general mistrust of white men; only the names remain of the time when the courage and the adventure of Spain was an inspiration to Europe.

French explorers, some centuries later, had followed the proud dons, and they, too, had cruised among the islands under the command of Count La Pérouse. But the ships had struck one of the hidden coral reefs, and, for the most part, the crews fell victim to the sharks and to the natives. Some, more fortunate, if one can use so doubtful an expression, entrenched themselves in a less-inhabited part of the island. The natives feared them, calling them ship-spirits, and declaring they had noses two hands long before their faces, which were in reality the cocked hats that they still wore. These stranded sailors, after making a ship from wreckage and what implements they could secure, sailed away into the unknown, and were never heard of again.

But Coley is impatient to get to the islands all this while, so let us haul up the anchors of the *Southern Cross*, and carry him away to start his fishing in these strange waters.

CHAPTER VII

COLEY PICKS UP SOME NEW FRIENDS

YOU will remember that Bishop Selwyn's plan had been to cruise about among the islands persuading any young natives to come on board and travel to Auckland, in New Zealand, for education. Already some from almost every group of islands had made the venture: they had stayed for a while at St. John's College, and, at the next voyage, had returned home. On this first cruise of the *Southern Cross*, they hoped to get together a good company of natives, who could travel to New Zealand in all the comfort of a specially-arranged mission ship. Although the journey was full of danger, it was interesting to make new friends and to hunt up the old ones on the islands.

Bishop Selwyn and his party had greeted the settlers of Norfolk Island, they had stayed with the Scotch missionaries of Anaiteum, and now, after passing Erromango, they made a cautious approach to Faté, which still kept its bad character for cannibalism. Out shot the canoes to meet them, gathering thickly about the ship, but apparently in a friendly spirit, and giving no cause for alarm.

"The first canoe that came had five men on board," so runs Coley's journal. "Girdles of beautifully-plaited cocoa-nut fibre round their waists were their only clothing, but some had wreaths of flowers and green leaves round their heads, and most of them wore mother-of-pearl shells, beads, etc., round their necks and in their ears. They do not tattoo but brand their skins. All five came, and presently three more, and then another; but seeing a large double canoe, with perhaps twenty men in her, coming close, we stood away. Two of our visitors chose to stay, and we have them on board now — Alsoff, a man of perhaps forty-five, and Mospa, a very intelligent young man, from whom I am picking up words as fast as I can. Fanny would have laughed to have seen me rigging them out in calico shirts and buttoning them up. Mospa gave me his wooden comb, which they push through their hair. Another fellow, whose head was elaborately frizzled and plastered with coral lime, departed with one of my common calico pocket-handkerchiefs, with my name in Joan's marking."

The Faté men, Coley's first captures, soon made themselves at home on board and slept that night in fine style, wrapped in a couple of blankets and cuddling close up to Coley himself.

Coley had made friends with his first cannibals, and he was now to be introduced to one of the trading pirates, whose cruel trade was the pest of the South Seas.

"*July 21.* — All day we have been very slowly drifting

Fanny would have laughed to have seen me rigging them out in calico shirts

along the west side of Espiritu Santo. A grand mountainous chain runs along the whole island; the peaks we estimate at 4,000 feet high. This alone is a fine sight — luxuriant vegetation to nearly the top of the peaks, clouds resting upon the summit of the range.

"... As we were lying to, about halfway up the coast, we espied a brig at anchor close inshore. Manned the boat and rowed about two miles to the brig. Found it was under the command of a man notorious among the sandalwood traders for many a dark deed of revenge. At Nengonè, he shot three in cold blood who swam off to his ship because the people of the place were said to be about to attempt to take his vessel. At Malicolo, but lately, I fear, he killed not less than eight, though here there was some scuffling and provocation. For the Nengonè affair, he was tried for his life at Sydney, Captain Erskine and the bishop having much to do with his prosecution. He is now dealing fairly (apparently) with these people and is certainly on very friendly terms with them... We are glad to let these men see that we are about in these seas, watching what they do; and the bishop said: 'Mr. Patteson has come from England on purpose to look after these islands.'"

Beyond the brig, and in the natural harbour made by a bend in the coral reef, Coley and the bishop made their landing. Breadfruit trees, coconut palms, and bananas grew in great quantities, and numberless brown babies left their splashing in the water to stare at the newcomers.

"There was no shyness on the part of the children, dear

little fellows from six to ten clustering around me, unable to understand my coat with pockets and what my socks could be — I seemed to have two or three skins. The men came up and soon shook hands but did not seem to know the custom. A Nengonè man was ashore, and with him, I could talk a little. Soon I was walking on shore, arm in arm, with him stark naked. A little boy of the island held the other hand, and so, leaving the boat, we walked inland into the bush to see a native village. Ten minutes' walk brought us to it — cottages all of bamboos tied together with coconut fibre, thatched with leaves, a ridge pole, and sloping roof on either side reaching to the ground.

"... They have plenty of pigs and dogs, which they eat, and some fowls. Spears I saw none, but bows and arrows. I took a bow out of a man's hand and then an arrow and fitted it to the string; he made signs he shot birds with it. Clubs they have, but, as far as I saw, only used for killing pigs."

Coley could not stay very long anywhere, so they were off and away again to other islands, where the sea was "lined with coral — purple, blue, scarlet, green, and white," with "little blue fishes, the bright blue starfish, the little land crabs walking away with other people's shells." At Bellona, where they landed, the chief wanted the ribbon from Coley's hat. "So I let him take it," writes Coley, "which he did by putting his adze against it, close to my ear, and cutting it off — not the least occasion to be afraid of them." Bishop Selwyn was always alert and watchful, however, and if there was any suspicion of danger, he would whisper a quick "Come along," and together they would swim back to the boat.

Wherever they went, they would barter fishhooks, hatchets, and adzes, or even pieces of calico, in exchange for food. This consisted of yams — a sort of sweet potato — breadfruit, bananas, and occasionally a pig or a fowl. The natives even confused the words "bishop" and "fishhook," thinking that, of course, they must have the same meaning since they were always found together. It must have been a curious market with a bishop bartering for a pig, while its owner, a man with eight or nine pieces of wood sticking out of his nose like a cat's whiskers, was debating whether he would take an adze or a hatchet in exchange.

At Malicolo, the old chief Melambico recognised Bishop Selwyn and called to him to land, so it was considered safe to row into shore. Here, the bishop read out the names of those he had known on former visits to the islands, while the crowd that gathered around them called out, "Dead," or "Shot"; so it seemed as if some war between the tribes had taken place. Nipati, one of the natives, stood meanwhile beside Coley, as curious about his dress as Coley was over the tortoiseshell earrings and shell armlets, the feathered and poisoned arrows, and the black and red stripes that decorated his companion. At Vanikoro, the inhabitants had fled at their approach, leaving behind the hideous fragments of a cannibal feast.

All this time, the *Southern Cross* had been gathering passengers from almost every island — men and boys, and even a few women and children, who soon learned to follow Coley about like dogs, "holding their hands in mine as a little child does with its nurse." It was now time to voyage homewards, and so the *Southern Cross*, with her motley crew on board, headed for Auckland Harbour, where she arrived on September 13, after a cruise of four months and a half.

CHAPTER VIII

COLEY TURNS SCHOOLMASTER

ALONG, low line of white buildings, not unlike an English farmstead, would be your first idea of the schoolhouse in New Zealand, where Coley was to teach his native boys. Not much like a college, if you have Oxford or Cambridge in your mind. In fact, it was more like a farm altogether in those days, when schoolmasters and scholars had to busy themselves as much with the farm work as with lesson books, when milking and cooking were important parts of the order of the day. Many of the island boys had never seen an animal bigger than a pig; they danced and chattered round the cows and horses with a delight not entirely free from fear; and they were so astonished over all the new sights and scenes that it must have been a hard job to get them to work.

They did not look exactly like Eton boys; in fact, until Coley began to dress them, their morning toilette began and ended with their hair. A Futuma boy was careful, for instance, to twist grass and coconut fibre in and out of his hair, plastering the whole very elaborately with coral lime. As his hair grew, he had only to add a little more to the binding, until at last it stood out any distance around and away from his head. Then he would crimp and curl the ends like a poodle's coat. Other islanders preferred bead and bone ornaments to the grass and coconut fibre; and there was a distinct difference of opinion as to whether black or red paint, or both used alternately, were the best decorations for the face. Yet others preferred to keep their hair comparatively free from decorations, while they spent their energies in letting large bone ornaments into their noses and ears; and they all hung bead, shell, or mother-of-pearl necklaces round their necks.

It must have seemed to Coley as if he were keeping school in a nightmare, especially as the boys from the different islands all talked different languages, and they were not all equally agreeable when their bows and poisoned arrows were taken away from them.

As a rule, Mr. Headmaster Coley had been obliged to dress his scholars on the homeward voyage. If you care to look at your map, the tropic line is drawn through the heart of the islands, while New Zealand lies some distance to the south, and is consequently much colder; for, in that upside-down world, south means cold, and north means hot. Coley had become an excellent tailor as well as a daring sailor; in fact, he was fast qualifying for all the professions that the cherrystones might promise him. He cut out trousers and stitched up shirts; and though, perhaps, Eton might not have given him very large orders, Melanesia became as proud of its new clothes as the celebrated emperor himself. In fact, a poor Nengonè dandy wrote a very sad letter on his slate to Coley, who had accused him of keeping his best trousers to take home with him to Nengonè.

"Mr. Patteson — this is my word — I am unhappy because of the word you said that I wished for clothes. I have left my country. I do not seek clothes for the body. What is the use of clothes? Can my spirit be clothed with clothes for the body? Therefore my heart is greatly afraid; but you said I greatly wished for clothes, which I do not care for."

The poor fellow was evidently much distressed, but all the time he probably loved his best trousers more than anything else in the world.

Coley kept his half-year school at St. John's, Auckland, for three or four years; but the air was too cold for the delicate islanders, and they had to move to St. Andrew's, Kohimarama, a school built on the shores of the harbour below from the profits of the "Daisy Chain," a book you may possibly know. Some years later they had to move school again, and this time the missionary centre was practically fixed in Norfolk Island. But wherever the school was held, the day's work and the day's play were very much the same.

Headmaster Coley was up at five every morning, pulling the blankets off sleepy boys with ever so many jokes and ever so much laughter. At meal time, the whole strength of the company met together and ate together, and the savage lads had to learn the mysterious uses of chairs and tables, knives and forks. After breakfast, they were told off to their different employments, each going, according to his turn, to work with his brain, or to work with his hands. Coley himself never liked teaching, even though he was clever enough at learning languages. In fact, he learnt so many and so quickly that at last he could talk no less than twenty-three, and had written and printed the grammars of thirteen. It is almost dreadful to think of so many grammars. It is almost difficult to think of a real, actual hero making grammars! Yet when you say over the quaint names, they sound more interesting. It would be rather nice to be able to talk Vun Marama, Api, Anudha, or Mãra-Masiki!

Coley had come a long way from home on a very special mission, and so he began at once to teach the boys about the Love of God. It was easy to make it plain and simple for them. They could see how much he loved them, so it was not hard to explain the mightier Love of God. They knew how willing Coley was to help them, so he could pass on and tell them of the true help that came from Heaven itself in the person of our Blessed Saviour. As they learnt that goodness and peace came from God, they began to understand that hatred and warfare grow from sin.

This lesson was the foundation on which Coley began to build. As children of God, the savage boys had to learn to be honest, pure, self-controlled, self-respecting. It is not easy to teach the lazy savage folk that work is an honourable thing. South Sea islanders are quite content to sit for hours upon the beach with nothing to do but gossip. This had all to be changed for brisk work — not only "fagging" for the white men but working side by side with them; taking a fair share of the burden, and earning fair wages as reward.

All work and no play would make as dull a boy out of a savage as out of an English Jack. There had to be play in plenty, with all the jolly give-and-take of English games. There was, of course, cricket, even if it were not exactly the sort approved of by Lillywhite; there was boating, football, and fishing. Indoors, the game of draughts so captivated some of the men that they sat playing all day while the women were left to do the work. Then came a word or two about "duty" in Coley's Sunday sermon, with the result that John Cho burnt his draughtboard as an act of renunciation.

A donkey proved a very great attraction to the boys, and Coley describes their attempts to ride it with keen enjoyment: -

"No one of them can retain his seat for more than ten minutes; but they all fall like cats on their legs, amid screams of laughter. The donkey steers straight for some scrubby trees, and then kicks and plunges, or else rubs his legs against the sides of the house, and all the boys are leaping about the unfortunate fellow who is mounted, and the fun is great."

The great trouble that overshadowed this happy school

life was the constant illness among the boys. Hardly a day passed without Coley having one of his scholars cuddled up in his own room in need of special care.

One year, indeed, a dreadful sickness visited the little community. The friendly dining-hall that had been the centre of so much happiness and hospitality had to be hastily turned into a hospital. Coley had been missionary, ship's captain, builder, baker, tailor, cook, and farm-hand, and now the sadder task of doctor and nurse lay before him. He had no sleep for a fortnight or more as he moved about among his boys, nursing them with his own tender hands, watching by them and comforting them. Alas! Too often he had to carry the slight, frail bodies of those who died in his own arms, and with a breaking heart, to their resting-place in the little churchyard. These are times that snatch the fun and brightness from a man's life, and leave behind the heavy trace of sorrow in anxious furrows and grey hair.

After Coley had been a schoolmaster for a bit, he had his first experience of living quite alone among savages, and this happened in 1858, when he left New Zealand in the *Southern Cross* to make his headquarters in the island of Lifu.

CHAPTER IX

COLEY SPENDS THREE MONTHS AT LIFU

"S ETTLED that I stop at Lifu in the interval between *"April 12.* the two voyages. I think Lifu wants me more than any other island just now. Some 15,000 or 20,000 stretching out their hands to God. I can't go for good, because I have, of course, to visit all the islands; but I shall try to spend all the time that I am not at sea or with boys in New Zealand, perhaps three months yearly, with them, till they can be provided with a regular clergyman.

"So I shall have no letters from you till the return of the vessel to pick me up in September. But be sure you think of me as very happy and well cared for, though, I am glad to say, not a white man on the island; *lots* of work, but I shall take much exercise and see most of the inhabitants."

"… I take a filter and some tea. We shall have yams, taro, cocoa-nuts, occasionally a bit of turtle, a fowl, or a bit of pork. So you see I shall live like an alderman; I mean if I am to go to every part of the island, heathen and all. I say heathen and all, because only a very small number of the people now refuse to admit the new teaching... So now I have parochial charge for three months of an island about twenty-five miles long and some sixteen or eighteen broad."

Coley's next abiding-place was a lath-and-plaster hut, built by one of the Samoan teachers who had been helping the people in Lifu as far as he was able, though only about fifteen had been actually baptized. The four rooms that composed the hut were well occupied: perhaps one of our good sanitary inspectors might have considered it *too* well occupied. Coley and four boys slept in one room, eight lads in another, the teacher Tutoo and his wife in the third. A fourth room was meeting-place, college, dining-room, and hall, whither the neighbours would wander, urged by curiosity, or because they had nothing to do.

The rough coral rocks of Lifu were not very fertile, and yams were the chief part of Coley's diet — not a nourishing food for an Englishman who, like the old lady of nursery fame, "would never keep quiet." These yams were bought each morning according to a fixed rate of exchange. Coley secured enough for his housekeeping, and the savage was able to possess a coveted pair of trousers, some calico, some fish-hooks, or a tomahawk. Food and cooking were two of Coley's chief difficulties, especially in the case of the constant illness that attacked the delicate and consumptive natives.

"Poor people," he wrote. "I wish I could contrive

some remedy for the dry food, everything being placed between leaves and being baked on the ground, losing all the gravy; and when you get a chicken it is a collection of dry strings. If I could manage boiling; but there is nothing like a bit of iron for fireplace on the island, and to keep up the wood fire in the bush under the saucepan is hard work... If I had studied the practical – bled, drawn teeth, mixed medicines, rolled legs perpetually, it would have been worth something... Every missionary ought to be a carpenter, a mason, something of a butcher, and a good deal of a cook."

Coley had often long distances to cover over the loose sand and the rough coral in order to visit his sick folk on the more distant parts of the island. Once they were threatened with a large importation of very degraded French convicts, whom the French Government wanted to ship to Lifu. Then Coley journeyed off to the other side of the island to interview a French priest who had been sent to prepare for their coming, for he was most anxious to save the islanders from such unsatisfactory guests.

"Off we set — two miles of loose sand at a rattling pace, as I wanted to shake off some 200 people who were crowding about me. Then, turning to the west, climbed over some coral rocks very quickly, and found myself with only half my own attendants and no strangers. Sat down, drank a cocoa-nut... and went on the remaining eight or nine miles to Zebedee's place, a Samoan teacher. They were very attentive, and gave me some supper. They had a bed which was, of course, given up to me in spite of opposition. They regard a missionary as something superhuman, almost. Sometimes I can't make them eat or drink with me. Then fifteen miles over to Apollo's place on the west coast, a grand bay with perfectly calm water, delicious in the winter months. Slept at Apollo's. Next morning went a little way in canoes, and walked six miles to Toma's place: meeting held, speech as usual, present of yams, pig, etc. Walked back the six miles, started in double canoe for Gaicha, the other side of the bay; wind foul, some difficulty in getting ashore." Walked by the bad path to Apollo's... Walked twenty miles back to We, where I am now writing. Went the twenty miles with no socks: feet sore and shoes worn to pieces, cutting off leather as I came along. Nothing but broken bottles equals jagged coral. Paths went so that you never take three steps in the same direction, and every minute trip against logs, coral hidden by long leaves, and weeds trailing over the path. Often for half a mile, you jump from one bit of coral to another. No shoes can stand it, and I was tired, I assure you. Indeed, for the last two days, if I stopped for a minute to drink a nut, my legs were so stiff that they did not get into play for five minutes or so."

Besides these constant journeyings, which wore out all Coley's boots and left his feet so sore and blistered that he could hardly walk, he had a great deal of teaching to do. The island chief was quite a young lad named Angadhohua, and Coley tried, by increasing the respect paid to him, to make him feel some of the responsibilities of his position. Coley became, in fact, a sort of Prime Minister to the young chief, and helped and taught him his duties as a ruler.

With the beginning of September, Coley began to look out for the return of the *Southern Cross.* The bishop had promised to fetch him in four months, and the four months were over. His slender store of extra provisions, such as coffee, sugar, and biscuits, had come to an end, and he was entirely reduced to native fare. There was no fresh water on the island — another great privation — and Coley could only drink the little that collected in the holes among the coral rocks, and it always tasted more or less salt. This began to tell upon his health, besides the strain of hearing no news from home or the outside world.

When the ship at length arrived, Coley learnt that she had struck a coral reef after leaving him in Lifu, and had been in dock ever since, and so had been nearly a month overdue. Before the return to Auckland, another short voyage was made to the more friendly islands in search of scholars, with the result that on starting homewards once more they had sixty-three souls on board. There were no private quarters, except for the master, the mate, and crew. The remainder of the ship was divided into two large cabins, divided by light calico curtains into compartments. Coley was in charge of one cabin and forty-five Melanesians, sleeping with them on mats and blankets spread upon the floor. Bishop Selwyn took charge of the married couples and the children.

Thus home to Auckland and to letters, with their news of Feniton and the sisters, and his dear old father the judge, and all that he held so dear and missed so much.

CHAPTER X

COLEY LIVES ON SUGARLOAF ISLAND

COLEY changed his home as often as a gipsy; and the most likely address for his letters might well have been "Somewhere or other in the Southern Seas." Very soon after his return from Lifu, another plan was made for another four months' residence on yet another island. This time he chose Mota, or Sugarloaf Island, as a good centre for work.

Coley had already been there once or twice, and had always determined to live there sooner or later. The island rose up out of the sea just like a sugar-loaf, and it had many advantages. The soil was dry; there was a clear spring of fresh water; and a most splendid banyan tree, that spread out its many branches a good twenty paces round, had caught his fancy. The natives were bright and alert, and, according to the Melanesian standard of beauty, they were a handsome race.

Coley took with him a companion named Dudley, so that he would neither be quite so overworked nor quite so lonely as before. His heart was heavy notwithstanding when he left Auckland in May 1860, for the last letters from England had brought grave accounts of his father, who was lying hopelessly ill, and Coley was sailing away into a silence that might never be broken again.

The first thing to do at Mota was to build a house. The framework had been brought from Auckland, and enough land was bought to build it on by the solemn and legal exchange of a certain number of hatchets. The site chosen was the great banyan tree itself, under the shelter of which the little house was raised. Peter Pan built just such another house for his Wendy bird. The walls were of bamboo tied together, the thatch of cocoa-nut leaves bound and interwoven; and just outside the door were cocoa-nuts and breadfruit trees sloping down to the coral beach and the clear, blue sea.

The Mota people were a wilder set than the Lifu folk. Their strange heathen customs had still a firm hold upon them, and sometimes upset the school that Coley held under the banyan tree. One day an old fellow came wandering round the enclosure, and, slipping in when Coley was not looking, he planted a red flowering shrub within the fence. This must have seemed like a kindly contribution to the garden, until the scholars suddenly all got up and left the school and took themselves off without any intention of returning. So Coley had to hunt up the old gentleman and get him to explain that the plant was a charm, and then, after a great deal of persuasion, he was allowed to take the plant away, and the boys came back to school.

Peter Pan built just such another house

The day's work in Mota was always carefully planned out. Lessons took up the whole morning, and the scholars came or not as they chose; in the afternoon there was a long walk to some distant village, when, as a rule, Coley and his companion took different directions, only meeting in the late evening to report and compare notes before turning in.

One day Coley, attracted by the sound of drums, found his way to the village of Tasmate. Men, women, and children were gathered together in large groups outside the small houses, and many people seemed to be preparing food in flat wooden dishes. The drummers, in the middle of a group of men, were thumping away at their oblong wooden drums with a couple of short sticks, and an old man accompanied them on a strange wooden instrument.

A sacred stone had been arranged on a platform of earth and decorated with six or eight pigs' jaws, with the long, curling tusks still left in them, and in front of the stone were three poles covered with flowers and leaves. "About the middle of the ceremony," Coley writes in his journal, "an old, tall, thin man, with a red handkerchief — our gift at some time — round his waist, began ambling round the space in the middle of the houses, carrying a boar's skull in his hand." It was a weird, fantastic scene, especially as the sky was already darkening with heavy storm clouds, and at last, down came the tropical rain and ended the feast somewhat abruptly.

The island folk soon grew very fond of the white men.

They began to give up the charms by which they used to destroy one another. So firmly, indeed, had they believed in the charms that men were really struck dead through fright and superstition. One disastrous old chief, named Bula, of Nengonè, used to curse people to death, and they actually died, as it seemed, at his bidding. If one of his fifty-five wives offended him, she was cursed and died immediately. It is impossible to understand, but such things really happened.

Every village in Mota tried to keep Coley entirely to itself and sometimes even put his life in danger through their jealousy of the others. Once, coming suddenly through the bush, he stumbled into the middle of six men, with bows bent and arrows pointed directly at him. He called out, "All right," and all right it fortunately was, as these disconcerting savages had only come to protect him from the imaginary foes of another village.

"This is the very thing I told you not to do," said Coley, frowning, as he took the bow away from one of the men. "I tell you once more, if I see you take your bows again, though you may do it with a good intention towards me, I will not stay at your village."

Peter Pan's hut was pleasanter to look at than to live in. Bare boards instead of bedsteads, rough native food, the anxiety over his work, and the thought of his father began to make Coley ill. A bad gathering formed in his ear; he could not sleep, and it was a rare trial to his patience to bear with the loafers who strolled in from the village to loll about and gossip when the pain was at its worst.

Once more, all his special stores were used up. Wine, coffee, biscuits, and chocolate had all come to an end. The *Southern Cross* was due and overdue, and still no news came from the outside world. All through the long September, Coley watched and waited. It was an unhealthy month of illness under the banyan tree. The calm waters and fertile scene mocked Coley as he struggled on, ill and out of spirits, with his preaching and teaching. Would the time never pass! Would relief never come?

Coley was watching one day by a poor dying woman in one of the squalid native huts. Men, women, boys, girls, and pigs crowded into the tiny, smoke-begrimed hovel; there was no peace and no quiet, except so far as Coley had the power to give it. And there, at last, the tidings came to him that a ship was in sight. She was not the *Southern Cross*; they could not tell that she was even friendly. But there she lay, be she trader or convict ship, and she would at least bring some news of the rest of the world. When at last she drew near and put into the little harbour, she proved to be the *Lillah*, and she brought the news of the total wreck of the *Southern Cross*. She had gone down on some rocks called the Hen and Chickens, off New Zealand; and, though she lay there almost uninjured in many fathoms of water, the slender resources of the Mission could not afford to pay for her salvage.

She was only a ship, after all, and luckily no lives were

lost — and yet Coley had grown to love, with an almost human love, the quick, responsive little vessel that had answered so readily to his thought and guidance. The *Southern Cross* had become part of his work, and so part of his life. She was just exactly what he wanted, for she had been made and designed for his work. And now she was gone!

With a sinking heart, the party embarked on board the *Lillah*, that had been chartered to bring them home, and they found her but a wretched substitute for the *Southern Cross*. Trouble followed them. The next day, Mr. Dudley had severe sunstroke, and three native boys were taken dangerously ill. For a little while, it seemed as if all Coley's faith and prayer could avail nothing and that all must die.

The wind was contrary, the ship unhandy and more than uncomfortable. It was almost unbearable. One of the boys died, and his body was committed to the sea. There is just one picture that we have of Coley in all this trouble and misery, in a letter written home by Mr. Dudley. He stands there in the corner of the cramped and dreary hold, the sick are round him, and they have none to turn to but him. His gentle, sorrowful voice prays with them and for them or speaks the calm, familiar words of the Church prayers. Is it possible that Coley ever played cricket at Lord's? We begin to wonder if he has any self left.

CHAPTER XI

COLEY BECOMES A BISHOP

THERE are a great many names for a bishop, and a great number of titles. He may be called My Lord and the Right Reverend; he is a Doctor of Divinity, and, on all showing, a great man. But there is one beautiful name by which a bishop may be known, and that is a Father in God.

When the people in England, and the people of Australasia, determined on making Coley a bishop, we like to think of him best as bearing the last and the most beautiful title. He had been a capital son all along, and a really helpful brother, and now that he was older, he was to be given a special spiritual fatherhood over his dusky South Sea islanders.

The idea had been talked over some time before, but it was only on arriving in New Zealand from Mota that Coley found many of the arrangements already made. He was too humble to accept such a position boldly, and he was also too humble to refuse it; "for," he said simply, "the Church of England will recognise me as one who stands in special need of grace and strength from above."

At Feniton, the two sisters busied themselves at once

over Coley's new clothes. Coley made merry over this view of the matter. "Dear Joan is investing money in cutaway coats, buckles without end, and no doubt knee-breeches, and what she calls gambroons (whereof I have no cognisance), none of which will be worn more than four or five times in the year. Gambroons and aprons and lawn sleeves won't go a-voyaging, depend upon it." How kind and good of her to take all the trouble. I don't laugh at *that*, and at her dear love for me, and anxiety that I should have everything; but I could not help having a joke about gambroons, whatever they are."

St. Matthias' Day, February 24, was fixed for the consecration; and Coley drew near to this great change as calmly and steadfastly as he had met all the different happenings of his life. The consecrating bishops, Judge and Lady Martin, Mrs. Abraham, and Mr. Lloyd, met in the little chapel of Tarama, on the evening before, for prayers and a lesson, and finally the glorious outburst of "Gloria in Excelsis." When all was over, Bishop Selwyn walked across to where Coley was still kneeling. Then, taking his hands and looking straight into his eyes, he said: -

"I can't tell you what I feel. You know it — my heart is too full."

Coley could make no answer, for he dared not trust his voice. That night the moon lay full upon the harbour, turning the waters to silver. The calmness of the night was like a picture of Coley's own quiet faith. He walked slowly, gravely home to his lodgings at St. Stephen's Schools.

There was, as it were, a Presence surrounding him that covered all distances, and made both English home and heavenly home seem wonderfully near. "*Dominus tecum!*" ("The Lord be with you!"), said the Bishop of Wellington as he passed him on his walk, and then on to rest until the day broke. Then came the morning.

"I shall never forget the expression of his face," wrote Lady Martin to Fanny and Joan at home. "It was meek and holy and calm, as though all conflict was over and he was resting in the Divine strength. It was altogether a wonderful scene: the three consecrating bishops, all such noble-looking men, the goodly company of the clergy, and Hohua's fine, intelligent face among them, and then the long line of island boys, and of St. Stephen's native teachers and their wives, were living testimonies of mission work. Coley had told us in the morning of a consecration he had seen at Rome, where a young archdeacon had held a large illuminated book for the Pope to read the words of consecration. We had no such gorgeous dresses as they; but nothing could have been more simple and touching than the sight of Pagalana's young face as he did the same good office. There was nothing artistic about it. The boy came forward with a wondering yet bright look on his pleasant face, just dressed in his simple grey blouse."

Just for one moment, the calm was broken. Bishop Selwyn had loved Coley like a father; but away in England, his own true father, who had given him so generously to the mission, was thinking of him and praying for him on his consecration day. "I received this my son in the ministry of Christ Jesus," rang out Bishop Selwyn's voice in the sermon, "from the hands of a father of whose old age he was the comfort. He sent him forth without a murmur, nay, rather with joy and thankfulness, to these distant parts of the earth. He never asked to see him again, but gave him up without reserve to the Lord's work."

Then none dared look at Coley as he covered his face with his hands.

The consecration over, a Bible is given to the new bishop, and he is bidden both to read and to preach, to "hold up the weak, heal the sick, bind up the broken, bring again the outcasts, seek the lost." Coley, kneeling, received the Book, and it was the same Bible given him so many years ago by the old judge, the same Bible that he had spelled out so laboriously at five years old. Once again, the distance of years and of miles seemed to melt away, and Coley knew his father was quite close to him.

"How I held tight my Bible, that dear father gave me on my fifth birthday, with both hands, and the bishop held it tight too, as he gave me that charge in the name of Christ; and I saw in the Spirit the multitudes of Melanesia scattered as sheep amidst a thousand isles."

Coley had in very truth grown up, but he had had to grow up in many ways before he could take his place amongst the fathers of his Church. Growing had not been easy for him any more than it is for us.

"You will recollect," wrote the Bishop of Wellington, "that as a boy he was good, pure, and true as gold, but then he was very indolent, and, except at cricket or hockey, showed no signs of any energy or ability; and I fancy his career at Oxford was very similar. After his being admitted to a Fellowship at Merton, he seems, by his own account, to have had intellectual tastes stimulated by travel; but the repose of a small and petty curacy in Devonshire called out his best moral feelings, yet could hardly, I fancy, have developed much energy. All this natural disposition to repose makes the energy and devotedness of the last five years the more remarkable and the more evidently the work of grace and duty. Certainly, he is the most perfect character I have ever met."

CHAPTER XII

COLEY'S TRAVELS

COLEY had never any time to waste, and so very soon after his consecration he was off once again on a cruise to his islands. This time he had chartered the *Dunedin*: "the only vessel that I could make any arrangements about is known to be in such a state that the pumps are going every two hours," he writes in describing her. Still, she was put into sufficient repair for the voyage, though no amount of repair could have made her comfortable or suitable for his purpose.

Coley started in May, and thus missed the mails from England that were bringing him the tidings of his father's death. The sad news did not reach him until some months later, when he once more put in to Norfolk Island. Then he learnt how the old judge had lived to hear the full account of his consecration, and in his pride and joy had insisted on once again reading the evening prayers in the little household that he might pray for "John Coleridge Patteson, Missionary Bishop."

Fortunately, this grief was, for the present, kept from Coley, for grave trouble met him at Erromango. Only eighteen days before his arrival there, the two good Scotch missionaries, Mr. and Mrs. Gordon, had been put to death by the natives. A Nengonè lad called out the bad news across the water as they put in to the harbour, possibly in order to warn Coley himself. But Coley, knowing no fear, landed and, finding the graves of his old friends, he read the words of the Burial Service before he passed on to his work in other islands.

Sometimes it seems to us as if all the fun and gladness were shadowed out of the lives of the great men who really influence the world. Great sacrifice can alone make great heroes. Coley, however, had days of happiness and interest as well as such times of sorrow.

At each island where a landing could be hazarded, Coley would swim ashore, with a small basket containing articles for exchange with the natives round his neck. Every nerve and faculty must be alert and ready; for danger comes unawares, and when you are least prepared to meet it.

"It is a sharp sensation," Coley wrote in one of his letters, "sitting alone (say) 300 yards from the boat, which of course can't be trusted in their hands, among 200 or more people really gigantic. No men have I seen so large — huge Patagonian limbs, and great heavy hands clutching up my little weak arms and shoulders. Yet it is not a sensation of fear, but simply of powerlessness; and it makes one think of another Power present to protect and defend."

When Coley stayed a night on shore, he would find his

way to the Ogamal, or men's common eating and sleeping house. This is an immense shed, some seventy or eighty feet long, divided by log boundaries into different compartments. In each compartment is an oven surrounded by various pots and pans, and the men are only allowed to use the compartment that corresponds with their rank and position. The higher you go in life, the further you may move up in the Ogamal.

Men and boys are admitted, with weird and uncouth ceremonies, and no women or children are ever allowed in or near the place. Fees have to be paid for the corner secured to you in the shed, sometimes in shell money, sometimes (as you improve your position) in pigs. By degrees and with good fortune you might at last get to the top of the shed, for which privilege you would have to pay quite a number of pigs. It must have been rather like working your way up the line in Sir Roger de Coverley, only that it took ever so much longer.

Coley says he soon got accustomed to sleeping with thirty, forty, fifty naked fellows lying, sitting, sleeping round him. It would require some courage at first. The long, low, dark hut, with the dusky shadows coming and going so stealthily to their place, now approaching the mat where Coley lay, and bringing a cocoa-nut or some other food. But he could never tell, as they crept up to him, whether it might not be death that they brought.

"I did not much like the manner of some of the people," he wrote of Vanua Lava; "they did not, at night, come into the Ogamal, as before; and I overheard some few remarks which I did not much like — something about the unusual sickness being connected with the new teaching.

The next morning I started about eight, buying two small pigs for two hatchets, and yams and taro and dried bread-fruit for fish-hooks. As we pulled away, one man drew his bow. The man did not let fly his arrow; I cannot tell why this demonstration took place."

The natives have a great belief in ghosts, and very often when Coley landed they thought he was a ghost come back to visit them. Between the terror of spirits and the terror of their enemies, in some places the people hardly dared go outside their villages. They used to ask Coley if they might walk with him, and after going about two miles they would confess they had never ventured so far from home before. When a woman went to get water from a hole in the rock, her husband would follow her with bow and arrows in case she were attacked. They lived in perpetual fear of the terror by night and of the arrow that flieth by day.

In the island of Ysabel, a fierce and relentless war had driven the survivors of one tribe even into the trees for shelter and defence. There, like some great hawk, they built their dwelling-place in the topmost branches, ready to pounce, if need arose, upon their prey. The only means of approach were movable ladders, up which the men, women, and children ran as nimbly as monkeys, never making use of their hands either on the ladder or as they

They built their dwelling-place in the topmost branches

walked about upon the branches with their bare feet. This was the more wonderful, as the houses were often perched eighty or ninety feet above the ground.

Coley wanted very much to explore these birds'-nest houses; but after one of his native sailors had ventured and told him how difficult was the ascent, he thought discretion was the better part of valour, and explained to the people that as he had no wings he dared not risk a fall. Perhaps if he had gone he might have found Wendy helping Peter Pan with his spring clean. However, he stopped in a hut below.

"That night, as I lay ignominiously on the ground in a hut, I heard the songs of the women aloft as voices from the clouds, while the loud croaking of the frogs, the shrill noise of the countless cicadas, the scream of cockatoos and parrots, the cries of birds of many kinds, and the not unreasonable fear of scorpions, all combined to keep me awake."

It is said that when two villages, such as Mahaya and Hoqirano in Ysabel Island, have long been at war and wish to make peace, they plant a cocoa-nut tree and say that all warfare shall cease when the tree bears fruit. As this means at least seven years, it gives them still a pretty good chance of fighting it out.

Among the customs of the natives, which must have added to the terrors of their appearance, was the habit of chewing pepper-leaf, areca-nut, and lime. It made the mouth look unnaturally large; the great teeth turned black, and the lips oozed with a kind of red juice. It is a wonder that the babies in such a place ever dared look at their fathers and mothers. But the poor little things did not have very much chance.

Wherever Coley landed, and directly he was in the thick of the savages, the expression of his face would change. Always gentle and loving, a fresh look would come into it — the look of hunger and yearning, as if he were hungry and thirsty for the people. Mr. Tilly, who had actually left a real live man-of-war, *H.M.S. Cordelia*, in order to follow Coley and Coley's mission as captain of his mission ship, notices and records that look on Coley's face; while the poor savages were drawn to it notwithstanding all their suspicions and doubts.

Perhaps the most wonderful island that Coley ever sighted was the great, majestic volcano of Tinakula, that rose 2,000 feet straight up out of the sea; and probably, since there was no anchorage, sloped down as sharply below the water. When first he saw it, the volcano was in full eruption.

"About 7 to 9 a.m. we sailed round the island and saw the fiery appearance at night is not actually fire or flame, but caused by hot, burning stones and masses of scoria constantly falling down the sides of the cone, which on the lee side are almost perpendicular. It was grand to see the great stones leaping and bounding down the sides of the cone, clearing 300 or 400 feet at a jump, and spring-ing up many yards into the air, finally plunging into the sea with a roar, and the splash of the foam and steam combined."

The few inhabitants whom Coley afterwards found upon the island were grey with ashes and dust.

CHAPTER XIII

COLEY'S HARVEST

IT would not be fair to tell you Coley's life without asking you to be a little pleased with Coley's success. Black Coat has a hard and toilsome life, and sometimes, when all is ended, there are but few to be interested in his work. Red Coat is so splendidly brave as he waves his sword and kills the foe. Black Coat also marches into danger, but he tries to bring life to men instead of taking it away.

Coley was beginning to reap the harvest of his work. Slow and sure he set to work; slow and sure were the ingatherings. Heathen customs began to drift away like some dreary mist before the sunshine, but they did not disappear all at once; in fact, they have not nearly all disappeared even now.

Coley had made books for his people, the first they had ever seen, sometimes translated from English, sometimes made up by himself. The natives learned laboriously to read and write, and they began to have a great number of fresh *wants*. They liked to possess books, ink, and paper. Then came a burning desire for writing-desks or boxes in which to keep their treasures. The joy of possession made them begin to understand the dirt and misery of their uncomfy huts. Such beautiful writing materials ought to have worthier homes. They were just like the man who found a horseshoe and went to buy a horse to fit it. Then they began to clean their houses, and nobody knows how long that took, for they have not finished yet.

It is a curious part of getting civilized, that when you have no *wants* at all, you are in a bad way altogether and must be provided with some as soon as possible. And then you get far too many *wants*, and you have to begin to learn to give up and practice self-denial and a simple life. I suppose we never know where to stop.

The savages had begun to leave off being savage. They wrote out lists of the things they wanted the mission ship to bring them; and it was almost like your mother's list when she goes shopping at the stores. They began to leave off wanting other people's heads, but began to wish for cups and saucers, soap, and saucepans instead!

When the mission center was settled in Norfolk Island, the scholars would crowd into Coley's house begging to learn.

"Two young married women are sitting in my room now," Coley wrote in a letter. "I didn't call them in, nor tell them what to do. 'We didn't quite understand what you said last night.' 'Well, I have written it out; there it is.' "They took, as usual, the manuscript, sat down, just as you or anyone would do, at the table to read it, and are now making their short notes of it."

You have heard that Coley was a tailor, but when it

came to the marriages of his Christian scholars, he was a dressmaker too. He cut out the brides' dresses and taught some of his boys to stitch them together; then he carried them off home, just as the "trotter," or dressmaker's assistant, brings home your sister's new ball dress. What is more, he dressed the brides with his own hands, even as the princess of the fairy tale threw the nettle-woven garments over her brothers and turned them from swans into princes. Still, that was not all; for he hammered the wedding rings out of sixpences, until the mission enclosure was merry with the sounds of tapping and beating. Then, at the last, he once more turned bishop, married the young couples in the little chapel, gave them his fatherly blessing, and sent them off to start Christian homes in the savage islands.

These were the days of baptism at the stream as well as at the font; the candidates standing by the clear water, the crowd of onlookers pressing to the water's edge. These were the days when Coley would carry out the command of the Ascension Day Gospel that had first speeded him on his way. Sometimes the convert had to renounce singly and by name each hideous heathen custom that had made them so cruel and so wretched in the old days.

Sometimes, in the tiny Norfolk Island chapel, opening out of Coley's room, he would gather in a special, quiet harvest. The door would swing open, and the dusky shadows would slip in from the wealth of bright sunshine outside. "You cannot go into the chapel between 5 and

6:30 a.m. without seeing two or three kneeling in different corners."

Sometimes the door into Coley's room would open, and a little figure would steal in from the chapel.

"Hullo, Marosqagalo! What do you want?"

"Please write me my prayer," said the little fellow, crippled with rheumatism, who came in. He was not the only one. They would come in to pour out their temptations, sorrows, and troubles there in Coley's study, asking, through him, for the good help that never failed them.

Coley had his harvest in Confirmation and, best of all, when, in the early morning, he gave his children the Bread of Life with words of their own language that they could understand.

At last, on December 20, 1868, he was able to ordain one of his own boys as deacon in the mission. This was George Sarawia from Vanua Lava, who had joined Bishop Selwyn in the voyage of 1857. Little George was terribly frightened when first he ventured on the white man's ship, and when the evening prayers were said, he felt quite sure he was about to be killed. It is not difficult to imagine his fears among the strange faces, in a strange ship, and on the open sea. If the missionaries were brave, their scholars were wonderfully plucky too. But George lived to tell the tale; and perhaps he tells it now where he still lives, away in the distant Southern Seas.

Perhaps we can understand yet a little more of Coley's harvest and what it meant if we listen, as he speaks to

Walter Hotaswol from Matlavo, who is dying in Coley's house.

"I was sitting next to him when he said, à propos of nothing, 'Very good.'"

"What is very good, Walter?"

"The Lord's Supper!"

"Why do you think so?"

"I can't talk about it. I feel it here" (touching his heart). "I don't feel as I did."

"But you have long believed in Him?"

"Yes, but I feel different from that. I don't feel afraid for death. My heart is calm" (me masur Kal, of a calm following a gale).

"Presently —

"Bishop!"

"Well?"

"Last night — no, the night before I received the Lord's Supper—I saw a man standing there, a *tanum liana* (a man of rank and authority). He said, 'Your breath is bad; I will give you a new breath.'"

"Yes?"

"I thought it meant, I will give you a new life. I thought it must be Jesus."

CHAPTER XIV

COLEY STANDS FACE TO FACE WITH DEATH

As early as 1857, less than two years after his first arrival, Coley had been shot at by the natives of the island of Santa Maria. In fact, this particular island was known as Cock Sparrow Point, since the mission party was almost always speeded on its way with a parting arrow. But it was not until a great deal later, in 1864, that the first real disaster happened to the mission, and Coley was called to face death. In the event of an outbreak, they had always two dangers to dread: there might, as in the case of Mr. and Mrs. Gordon of Erromango, be instant and unexpected death, or, on the other hand, there might be the terrible long agony of dying from the wounds of poisoned arrows. Not very long after Coley had been working at Kohimarama, one of his boys had broken the rules and managed to regain possession of one of the arrows he had brought from his island home. Tohehammāi meant no harm, and had only taken the forbidden arrow with just a dash of fun, and just a bit of daring, in order to exchange it for a shirt belonging to an English boy. Boy-like, too, as he carried it off, he must needs play about with another stick, casting it like a spear before him as he went along. So, stooping once to pick it up, he pricked his elbow sharply against the point of the arrow. Nothing was said, no one was told, until after twelve days his arm stiffened. The poison had begun to work. Then came sudden twitchings in his arms, increasing to convulsions; his whole body grew rigid, and the throat contracted, so that he could no longer swallow. It was the horrible lockjaw, from which there was little or no hope of recovery. Coley tended the lad through the two days of his agony, and laid his body to rest when all was over. It was his first approach to the horror of such an illness, but off Santa Cruz, he was to have a nearer and a more bitter knowledge of it.

In May 1869, the mission party left Norfolk Island, with three excellent Norfolk Island men on board — Edwin Nobbs, Fisher Young, and Joseph Atkin — besides the small English crew. Never had they started under happier conditions, and a capital prospect for work lay before them. Erromango, Vanua Lava, Mota, Ambrym, and Malicolo were visited without any adventure. At Tariko, however, after landing in the usual place, they found to their consternation that it was the boundary between two rival tribes, who had each brought food for barter to the same spot. A bit of jealousy, a few words, and bows were strung and arrows flying. "I was in the middle," said the bishop; "one man only remained by me, crouching under the lee of the branch of the tree, and shooting from thence within a yard of me. I did not like to leave the steel-yard, and I had to detach it from the rope with which it was attached to the tree, and the basket, too, was half full of yams and heavy, so that it was some time before I got away, and walked down to the beach, and waded to the boat, shooting going on all round at the time; no one shooting at me, yet, as they shot on both sides of me at each other, I was thankful to get well out of it."

The boat at last made for the ship, the second Southern Cross, lately sent from England; and, for the moment, danger was averted, and all was well.

From Tariko they made for Parama and Sopovi, and thence, on August 15, they landed at Santa Cruz.

It was not until August 27, on Fanny's birthday, kept so calmly and so pleasantly at Feniton Court, that Coley gathered up courage to write about the dreadful days that followed.

"Dear Fan — You remember the old happy anniversaries of your birthday — the Feniton party — the assembly of relations—the regular year's festivity.

"... The day comes to me in the midst of one of the deepest sorrows I have ever known. On August 15 I was at Santa Cruz. You know I had a very remarkable day there three years ago. I felt very anxious to renew acquaintance with the people, who are very numerous and strong. I went off in a boat with Atkin (twenty), Pearce (twenty-three or twenty-four years old), Edwin Nobbs, Fisher Young, and Hunt Christian, the three last Norfolk Islanders. Fisher has been with me two or three years — all young fellows of great promise, Fisher, perhaps, dearest of all to me, about eighteen, and oh! so good."

I landed at two places among many people, and after a while came back as usual to the boat. All seemed pleasant and hopeful. At the third place I landed amidst a great crowd, waded over the broad reef (partially uncovered at low water), went into a house, sat down for some time, then returned among a great crowd to the boat, and got into it. I had some difficulty in detaching the hands of some men swimming in the water.

"Well, when the boat was about fifteen yards from the reef, on which crowds were standing, they began (why, I know not) to shoot at us. I had not shipped the rudder, so I held it up, hoping it might shield off any arrows that came straight, the boat being end on, and the stern, having been backed into the reef, was nearest to them.

"When I looked round after a minute — providentially, indeed, as the boat was being pulled right into a small bay on the reef, and would have been grounded — I saw Pearce lying between the thwarts, with the shaft of an arrow in his chest, Edwin Nobbs with an arrow, as it seemed, in his left eye, many arrows flying close to us from many quarters. Suddenly Fisher Young, pulling the stroke oar, gave a faint scream; he was shot through the left wrist. Not a word was spoken, only 'Pull, port oars! pull on steadily.' Once dear Edwin, with the fragment of the arrow sticking in his cheek, and the blood streaming down, called out, thinking even then more of me than of

I had not shipped the rudder, so I held it up,
hoping it might shield off arrows

himself, 'Look out, sir! close to you!' But, indeed, on all sides they were close to us.

"How any of us escaped I can't tell. Fisher and Edwin pulled on; Atkin had taken Pearce's oar, Hunt pulled the fourth oar. By God's mercy no one else was hit, but the canoes chased us to the steamer. In about twenty minutes we were on board: the people in the canoes round the vessel, seeing the wounded, paddled off as hard as they could, expecting, of course, that we should take vengeance on them."

"... I drew out the arrow from Pearce's chest; a slanting wound, not going in very deep, running under the skin, yet of apparently almost fatal character to an ignorant person like myself; 5½ inches were actually inside him. The arrow struck him in the centre of the chest and in the direction of the right breast... He breathed with great difficulty, groaning and making a kind of hollow sound; was perfectly composed, gave me directions and messages in case of his death. I put on a poultice and bandage, and leaving him in charge of someone went to Fisher. The wrist was shot through, but the upper part of the arrow broken off and deep down; bleeding profuse, of which I was glad; I cut deeply, much fearing to cut an artery, but I could not extract the wooden arrowhead. At length, getting a firm hold of the projecting *point* of the arrow on the *lower* side of the wrist, I pulled it through; it came out clean... I poulticed the wound and went to Edwin. Atkin had got the splinter from his wound; the arrow went in near the eye and came out by the cheekbone; it was well syringed. "This was on Monday, August 15. All seemed doing well for a day or two; I kept on poultices, gave light nourishing food, &c. But on Saturday morning Fisher said to me: 'I can't make out what makes my jaw so stiff.'"

You will not want to hear much about Coley's solemn watching as the horrible illness laid hold upon the lad of eighteen. Nelson, as he lay dying in the cockpit of the *Victory*, cried out his "Kiss me, Hardy," before his lips were silent forever. There, in the after cabin of the *Southern Cross*, racked by convulsion, a boy, yet none the less a hero, stammered his "Kiss me, Bishop," and in an agony fell asleep. Both heroes, though for one there might be a resting place in St. Paul's and the other an almost forgotten grave in the South Sea Islands; and there is, indeed, a sort of glorious comradeship in their dying.

Still, the terrors of death laid hold upon the ship. Fisher had died. "He was my boy; I loved him as I think I never loved anyone else," wrote Coley in the fresh agony of sorrow: Edwin and Pearce were to follow him. All the peculiar horrors of the illness must be gone through yet again and then again, until the blue, motionless sea received its dead.

Coley will not want us to pry into his sorrow. He writes home about it all, yet with a gentle reserve that almost makes one feel that letters are silent things. But his hair has grown white, and he feels he can never be young again. His feet are also on the way of sorrows, and the holy cross that he has to bear was fitly laid upon his shoulders at Santa Cruz.

CHAPTER XV

COLEY FIGHTS THE PIRATES

THE "thief ships" had become very daring at this time in the South Sea. Although the traders were supposed to buy stores of sandalwood by fair exchange with the natives, they usually managed their bargains so that it might be "Heads I win and tails you lose." If they could get the sandalwood without payment at all, they took the chance and made off with it—not without a scuffle and the murder of one or two natives.

Another trade had sprung up, another reason for the pirate ships to cruise among the islands. Far away in the same Pacific Ocean, a busy and fertile island was crying out for workpeople. The Fiji people made good and honest plans for the care of any natives who might wish to come; they promised to feed them, look after them, and send them back within five years. They made a further offer of eight pounds for any workman willing to come for a time to their island.

The owners of the "thief ships" thought of a new way to satisfy their greed. If they could bring laborers to Fiji, whether willing or unwilling, they would be able to seize the eight pounds, and that would pay better than sandalwood. No sooner thought than done. Putting in, therefore, to the calm bay within the coral reef, the captain brought out his treasures of tobacco, pipes, and drink in order that he might coax the natives on board. Already accustomed to the *Southern Cross*, the canoes would gather round fearlessly enough, and the dusky fellows scrambled aboard the ship to feast or barter to their hearts' content.

"That bishop of yours," said the captain, "is a bad man. He brings you no presents as we do. You had better give him up and make friends with us." Then the natives nodded and gathered closer, like moths round the candle or flies in a spider's web. And then the spider pounced. There was a scuffle on deck; the natives, caught unawares, were thrust down under hatches. The ship set sail, and the captives were carried to Fiji.

The rest of the islanders would close up round the fires at night to discuss the meaning of it all. Coley had taken men away with him, but they had come home again after a bit and all the better for their voyage. It only dawned upon them slowly that the "snatch-snatch ship" plied a different trade and cared no more for the men when the eight pounds had once been paid to them. Then, learning wisdom by experience, as the saying is, they refused to be coaxed or bribed on board the traders anymore.

Coley was always about the islands and could warn his flock against the wolves that were about. He told them of their danger and advised them to have no dealings with

The natives, caught unawares, were thrust down under hatches

the traders, so that next time they could cry out like the seven little kidlings in the old story: "We know you are not our mother, for your voice is too gruff and your paws are too rough."

But, like the seven little kidlings, the wolf was ready to look round for a disguise. Next time the ship put into port, there was no drink and no tobacco, but the wolf was there on deck dressed up like a missionary, with a book in his hand and words of welcome on his lips. No sooner had the natives come on board than the sailors seized them and flung them into their prison below.

Greed for gold makes evil cunning. The traders thought of one more plan to catch the islanders, but it is almost too horrible to tell you about.

The chiefs of some of the wildest islands were still very proud of the skulls of their enemies, with which they decorated their huts. They were head-hunters, and their hideous trophies were piled in a ghastly heap at their doorway to prove how many victories they had gained and how many foes they had slain. The traders, after buying the friendship of these chiefs with drink and tobacco, offered to bring them heads if they would help to steal men for Fiji.

From this island and that, the cry went up to Coley, "Avenge us, Bisopè, avenge us." Nine men had been murdered in one place, five or more in another; some islands were almost deserted for the number of men carried off and killed. One day a ship named the *Water Lily* put into an island harbor. The sailors, either white men or half-castes, attacked the native canoes and managed to capsize them, beating down the men who struggled in the water with oars and tomahawks. Those they captured were taken on board, and several were beheaded, their bodies thrown to the sharks.

The traders were no longer "thief ships" or "snatch-snatch ships." The natives had learned to call them "kill-kill ships."

The island men were torn by agony, suspicion, and excitement. Coley, who had been seriously ill, fell to the work of sending reports, petitions, and appeals to the Government at home, begging for protection for his help-less flock. Those who knew him at this time speak of him as an old man, bent and gray, but he was not really old. Had he been in England like your father or mine, he might have been still playing cricket, fishing, or shooting, or riding to hounds. Coley was old through the sorrows of his children, and his heart was almost broken as he watched his work undone.

One of Coley's earliest scholars had been a young chief named Peterè from the island of Mai or "Three Hills." Every year that the island was visited, Peterè's ready welcome was the first to greet them, and his hands the first to draw them through the surf to shore. Once more the *Southern Cross* put into Mai, and Coley waded ashore. No Peterè welcomed him. The groups of men who gath-ered on the coral beach looked at him suspiciously; they talked amongst themselves as if a grave secret rested on their minds.

"Where is Peterè?" asked the bishop. "He has not come to greet me."

"Peterè was dead," they answered gruffly, and saying no more, they took Coley to the village where he had lived. A great lamentation greeted the missionaries. "Peterè is dead, is dead," they cried. "Oh, Bisopè, Peterè is dead," and all around the cry of sorrow went up. Coley spoke what words of comfort he could, but still the sense of a greater misfortune hung over him, and though he questioned, he learned no more. At last, an old scholar came forward. "Peterè is dead, Bisopè," he said, weeping. "We will not deceive you; he is dead, but no sickness took him. It was a white man who shot him. Oh, Bisopè, it was a white man from a ship! Peterè is dead; he was shot in the forehead. Since you loved him, we will tell you. Peterè is killed."

Thus, in the confession of Peterè's death, the poor Mai folk confessed also their great love for Coley. Revenge against the white man was burning in their hearts; they had meant to take it; they had meant not to spare even Coley; but love was stronger than death, and love had prevailed — but it had prevailed for the last time.

CHAPTER XVI

COLEY GOES HOME

WITH his heart heavy with the sorrow of Peterè's death, Coley put away from Mai in the *Southern Cross* and headed for Santa Cruz, where he had heard there was a labour vessel ready to seize men by fair means or foul. The wind was light, and they could make no progress. Coley spent the long hours in prayer or meditation; the sorrows of his children kept him silent and grave.

"*Sept. 16, 1871*" (his journal runs): – "On Monday I go to Nukapu. I am fully alive to the probability that some outrage has been committed here. The master of the vessel whom Atkin saw did not deny his intention of taking away from there, or from any other islands, any men and boys he could induce to come on board. I am quite aware we must be exposed to considerable risk on this account. I trust that all may be well, and that if it be His will that any trouble should come upon us, dear Joseph Atkin, his father's and mother's only son, may be spared."

It was on September 20 that the Southern Cross anchored outside Nukapu. No canoes came out to greet them, so the Bishop had the boat lowered that he might row to shore. Five men were with him in the whale-boat: Joseph Atkin, a young priest from New Zealand; Mr. Brooke, another missionary; Stephen Paroniaro; James Minipa; and John Nonono, Melanesians; besides a lad named Joseph Watè, fifteen years old. They rowed quickly to the shore, and still no signs were made from the groups of natives on the beach.

"Shall we land, friends?" called Coley from the boat. The natives agreed but silently, only making signs of assent. Pulling to the reef, they were now joined by four or five canoes, and as the whale-boat could not cross the reef, Coley was given a place in a native canoe. With grave South Sea courtesy, a basket of bread-fruit and yams was offered to him as he took his place. Just as he was prepared to take it, Mr. Atkin fancied he heard the whisper of "Tabu." Sometimes savages will try to make an enemy touch a thing tabu or holy, that they may have an excuse to kill him. Coley took the basket with his gentle smile of thanks. Then there was a delay of some twenty minutes, and at last the canoe, with the Bishop and the two chiefs, Moto and Tanla, drew away to the beach.

The whale-boat did not follow but drifted near at hand, watching the Bishop land and pass out of sight into the bush. Perhaps half an hour had passed by, and they had made some attempt to talk to the natives in the other canoes, who were still keeping near, when suddenly the tall, dusky form of one of the men stood up in his canoe, and, drawing his bow, he cried out, "Have you anything like this?" and shot a yard-long arrow into the boat.

Thus suddenly, in the still quiet of a tropical midsummer day, when heaven and earth seemed so absolutely at peace, the end came, and the pent-up misery of the savages was let loose on the only men who tried to stand between them and their injuries.

In a moment, the air was thick with arrows. Minipa, Nonono, Mr. Atkin, and Stephen had all been wounded, and still, with tense nerve and muscle, gathering all the force they were capable of, they pulled back to the ship. *But the bishop was on the island alone.* "We are all hurt," were the words as they were lifted on board; but it could not keep them from the Bishop. Once more, after leaving those who had been most badly wounded, they prepared to row back to the island.

"We are going to look for the Bishop; are you afraid?"

The words were passed round, and from the mate, Mr. Bongarde, to fifteen-year-old Watè, it was the same answer:

"Afraid! Why should I be afraid?"

They must wait until the tide was high enough to carry them over the reef, and the waiting was an agony. At half-past four, it became possible to cross the reef, and the boat put out.

As they drew near, two canoes came out to meet them, and one cast the other adrift and paddled silently back to the beach.

"It is an ambush," whispered the mate.

"It is the Bishop," cried a sailor, but his voice broke.

Two canoes came out to meet them, and one cast the other adrift

The boat drew alongside, and only two words passed: "The body!" as they lifted the long form, wrapped in matting, from the boat.

Coley had gone home.

Not at Feniton, in the peace of the Devonshire garden, but somehow, and in a way we cannot fully understand, the old judge had got his little boy home again.

For the last time, Coley was brought to the *Southern Cross*, and they could look upon his face once more. He was smiling as if he had at last received his reward—the old smile that had played round his lips at Eton and that the sorrows of his islands had chased away, but in the last had been given back to him again. Across his breast lay a palm branch, which for the savage meant revenge, but for the Christian is ever the sign of victory. And the marks that he bore upon his body were five, even as his Saviour bore but five wounds upon the cross.

One more night at sea for Coley, one more night on the *Southern Cross*, and then in the morning, with faltering voice, Joseph Atkin committed his body to the deep.

It was the Sunday afterwards. At the little altar on the *Southern Cross*, Joseph Atkin celebrated the Holy Communion, and the words, "All those who have departed this life in His faith and fear," seemed to that little company to spell but the one name of John Coleridge Patteson. With the chalice still in his hands, and the words upon his lips, Joseph Atkin suddenly faltered and hesitated. The Mota men on board looked at each other; they knew what it meant: it was the poison of the arrow at work, and the cloud of death was lowering upon them yet again. Joseph and Stephen were to follow Coley through the gates of death, even as they had followed him so faithfully in life.

Far away in Norfolk Island, they were watching for the ship.

"It is here! It is here!" went up the cry, and there was a shouting and a racing as the schooner became visible.

"She will be in early to-morrow. We must get the rooms ready," were the glad words passed from one to another. "A holiday for the boys, of course. You must all be there to welcome the Bishop" — and then, in the light of morning, the troubled news: "Look at the flag! What does it mean? It is half-mast high!"

Then from the ship, from the shore, spread the news that the *Southern Cross* had brought home to Norfolk Island:

"Hush! Do you not know? Only Brooke has come back!"

THE END